IL SECONDO LIBRO DELLE CANZONI
A SEI VOCI (1575)

RECENT RESEARCHES IN THE MUSIC OF THE RENAISSANCE

James Haar and Howard Mayer Brown, general editors

A-R Editions, Inc., publishes six quarterly series—

Recent Researches in the Music of the Middle Ages and Early Renaissance,
Margaret Bent, general editor;

Recent Researches in the Music of the Renaissance,
James Haar and Howard Mayer Brown, general editors;

Recent Researches in the Music of the Baroque Era,
Robert L. Marshall, general editor;

Recent Researches in the Music of the Classical Era,
Eugene K. Wolf, general editor;

Recent Researches in the Music of the Nineteenth and Early Twentieth Centuries,
Rufus Hallmark, general editor;

Recent Researches in American Music,
H. Wiley Hitchcock, general editor—

which make public music that is being brought to light
in the course of current musicological research.

Each volume in the *Recent Researches* is devoted
to works by a single composer or to a single genre of composition,
chosen because of its potential interest to scholars and performers,
and prepared for publication according to the standards that govern
the making of all reliable historical editions.

Correspondence should be addressed:

A-R EDITIONS, INC.
315 West Gorham Street
Madison, Wisconsin 53703

RECENT RESEARCHES IN THE MUSIC OF THE RENAISSANCE • VOLUMES LVII and LVIII

Giovanni Ferretti

IL SECONDO LIBRO DELLE CANZONI A SEI VOCI (1575)

Edited by Ruth I. DeFord

A-R EDITIONS, INC. • MADISON

Library of Congress Cataloging in Publication Data:

Ferretti, Giovanni, b. ca. 1540.
   [Canzoni, voices (6), 2o libro]
   Il secondo libro delle canzoni a sei
voci (1575)

   (Recent researches in the music of the Renaissance,
ISSN 0486-123X ; v. 57-58)
   Italian words ; prefatory matter in English ;
words printed as text with English translations on p.
   Edited from the 1st ed. published: Venice :
Scotto, 1575.
   Includes bibliographical references.
   "Canzone models" : p.
   1. Part-songs, Italian.   I. DeFord, Ruth I.
II. Series.

M2.R2384   vol. 57-58   [M1582]   83-2773
ISBN 0-89579-167-6

Contents

Preface

The Composer and His Music

Giovanni Ferretti was born about 1540, probably in Ancona, Italy, where he held his first known professional position and signed the dedications of his second book of *canzoni a 5* (1569) and first book of *canzoni a 6* (1573). The dedications of his other publications were signed in Venice, where he may have gone only to see his works through the press. All his known positions were as *maestro di cappella* in various churches. He held the position at the Cathedral of Ancona in 1575, at Santa Casa in Loreto from 25 July 1580 to 17 June 1582, at Gemona from October 1586 to December 1588, at Cividale del Friuli in 1589, and again at Santa Casa in Loreto from 14 October 1596 to 24 October 1603.[1] The nature of his employment during the remaining years of his life is unknown. He must still have been living in 1609, however, since he contributed a madrigal to the anthology *Sonetti novi di Fabio Petrozzi romano, sopra le ville di Frascati* (Rome: Robletti, 1609; RISM 1609[17]), which contained music exclusively by living composers. Since the poet and several of the composers represented in this anthology were Roman, it is possible that Ferretti was in Rome at that time. There is no biographical record of him after 1609.

Ferretti composed some sacred music and a few madrigals, but his importance in the history of music rests primarily on his seven books of *canzoni* (five books *a 5* and two books *a 6*), which were published between 1567 and 1585.[2] The term "canzone," as he used it, originated as an abbreviated form of "canzone alla napolitana." His second book *a 6* is entitled "canzoni," while all his other books are entitled either "canzoni alla napolitana" or simply "napolitane."

Ferretti's *canzoni* were among the most popular and influential compositions of their time. The books went through numerous editions in Italy, and many individual *canzoni* were included in anthologies published north of the Alps (in Antwerp, London, and Nuremberg), where they continued to be reprinted as late as 1634.[3]

These works played a critical role in the evolution of secular music throughout Europe in the late sixteenth century. Prior to their appearance, there had been a clear distinction between the madrigal and the various lighter forms of Italian secular music, such as the *villanesca, villotta,* etc. The lighter forms featured unpretentious, quasi-popular texts and music, which contrasted sharply with the serious, literary texts and sophisticated music of the madrigal. Ferretti's *canzoni* combined stylistic features of both the lighter forms and the madrigal, creating a new style that was more complex and serious than the traditional lighter forms, but lighter than the traditional madrigal. They exercised a profound influence on both genres and contributed to the gradual breakdown of the distinction between them.

The most important of the lighter forms of the sixteenth century was the *canzone alla napolitana* (also called *villanesca, villanella, villotta alla napolitana,* or simply *napolitana*). This genre probably originated in the oral tradition of Neapolitan popular singers, but became fashionable in aristocratic circles in the 1530s and has been preserved in written versions created by poets and composers catering to the tastes of the upper classes. *Canzoni alla napolitana* were originally written in Neapolitan dialect, but by about 1560, they had lost most of their regional linguistic features, while retaining the popular flavor and the poetic and musical forms of the native Neapolitan song. Their texts were simple and light-hearted and were invariably in strophic form, with or without a refrain. Each strophe usually had three or four lines with a rhyme scheme of *abb* or *aabb*. The music was also strophic, with each strophe usually having an internal form of *aabcc* or *aabb*.[4] The *canzone alla napolitana* was composed for three voices, with the principal melody in the top voice; the lower two voices formed a subordinate accompaniment, often doubling the melody in parallel motion. Undisguised parallel fifths between the outer voices, which contributed to the rustic flavor of the music, were a typical feature of the style. The melodies were simple, autonomous tunes, and the rhythms were strong and lively.

In both its literary and its musical style, the *canzone alla napolitana* contrasted sharply with the typical sixteenth-century madrigal. Madrigal texts were written in standard Italian, not a regional dialect, and normally had at least some degree of literary respectability; many were genuinely great poetry.

They were usually in non-strophic forms, and those that were strophic always had a different musical setting for each strophe. The length of the whole text, or of each strophe of the text, was normally considerably greater than four lines. The music was usually written for four to six equally important voices and always followed the rules of academically correct counterpoint. The melodic style of each individual voice was often conditioned by its relationship to the other voices, and the rhythmic style was subtle and flexible, often including contrasts of rhythm among different, simultaneous voices.

Many composers active in northern Italy and other parts of Europe, including Willaert, Donato, and Lasso, arranged three-voice Neapolitan *canzoni* for four voices. They usually placed the melody of the original song in the tenor or the soprano in their arrangements. Occasionally, however, they treated the melody more freely, allowing it to migrate from one voice to another, using motives from it as a basis for short points of imitation, or alternating fragments of it with freely composed material. They removed the most blatantly rustic features of the style, such as the parallel fifths, but in general retained the formal structures and the essential spirit of the models.[5]

Most of Ferretti's *canzoni* are also arrangements of earlier, three-voice Neapolitan *canzoni*. Although models are known for only about half of them, most of the others are so similar in poetic and musical style that they are probably arrangements of three-voice pieces that are no longer extant.[6] Some, however, may be free compositions.

Ferretti's general techniques for arranging three-voice *canzoni alla napolitana* are similar to those of his predecessors, but he fused these techniques with influences from the madrigal, thereby making his arrangements considerably more complex than those of earlier composers. He was the first composer to arrange Neapolitan *canzoni* for five or six voices, rather than the customary four voices, and he used the larger number of voices to create more elaborate and varied textures than those found in works by his predecessors. He also included musical representation of specific words of the text in some of his *canzoni*. This technique was usually applied to words in the first stanza only (unless the words occurred in a refrain section) and occasionally made the music inappropriate for the remaining stanzas.[7] Although Ferretti (or his publisher) included all stanzas of each text in his first four books of *canzoni a 5* (published 1567–71), the word-painting makes strophic performance undesirable in some of them, and only the first stanzas of originally strophic texts were included in his two books *a 6* (1573 and 1575) and his fifth book *a 5* (1585).

Because of the similarity of his arrangements of *canzoni alla napolitana* to madrigals, Ferretti was able to include a few genuine madrigals, as well as several types of light music, in his *canzone* collections without making the collections stylistically inconsistent. He did not usually give individual labels to the different types of pieces, but included all of them under the general title of "*canzoni*" or "*canzoni alla napolitana*."

Ferretti's *canzoni* initiated a tremendous vogue for pieces lighter and simpler than the traditional madrigal, but more subtle and complex than the traditional lighter forms. Following his example, many composers of lighter forms in the 1570s and 1580s (including Alessandro Merlo, Girolamo Conversi, Lodovico Agostini, Jacob Regnart, and Claude Le Jeune) scored their pieces for five or six voices. Even composers (such as Luca Marenzio and Orazio Vecchi) who preferred the more traditional three- or four-voice textures for the lighter forms often incorporated madrigalesque textures and musical representation in their lighter-form compositions. At the same time, many madrigal composers adopted some of the characteristic features of the *canzone* style, including light-hearted texts, repeated outer sections, and sprightly rhythms. These features are exemplified most clearly in the madrigals of composers such as Ruggiero Giovannelli and Felice Anerio, but can also be seen in many of the later madrigals of Andrea Gabrieli and the early ones of Marenzio and Monteverdi.

Composers in Italy continued throughout the century to distinguish madrigals from *canzoni* (which they also called "*canzonette*," "*villanelle*," etc.) in the titles of their publications, but by about 1580, the difference between a light madrigal and a complex *canzone* had, in fact, virtually disappeared. Anthologies of Italian music published outside of Italy after that date often included pieces originally published under both titles, without making any distinction between them.

Il secondo libro delle canzoni a sei voci

Ferretti's *Secondo libro delle canzoni a sei voci* contains twenty-one pieces, one of which is anonymous (labeled "*d'Incerto*" in the source). Of all his *canzone* collections, this one is the closest in style to the madrigal, in that it contains more actual madrigals than any other collection, and the lighter genres in it are more heavily influenced by the madrigal style. Significantly, it is the only one that does not include the designation "*alla napolitana*" on the title page. The designation "*tavola delle napolitane*" does appear in the table of contents, but it is probably the publisher's term, rather than Ferretti's.

The collection was first published in 1575 by the heirs of Girolamo Scotto in Venice. It was successful enough to be reprinted three times (in 1579, 1581, and 1586), and several numbers from it were also included in north-European anthologies. (Specific information on the editions is given below in the section The Edition.)

The dedicatee of the book was Giacomo Boncompagni, the son of Ugo Boncompagni (Pope Gregory XIII, 1572–85) and an important patron of musicians. Giacomo was appointed General of the Church by the pope in 1573 and was then promptly sent to Ancona, ostensibly to prepare to defend that city against a possible attack by the Turks, but actually to avoid criticism of nepotism by reform-minded members of the Curia.[8] Ferretti was in Ancona in 1573 and had become *maestro di cappella* of the cathedral there by the time he published this book in 1575; his relationship with Boncompagni probably dates, therefore, from sometime between 1573 and 1575.[9]

The opening piece in the book is a dedicatory madrigal referring to the joy people felt at the return of Boncompagni. It was probably composed to celebrate his return to Ancona from a trip to northern Italy in 1574. The pope had sent him there, along with his cousin, Cardinal Filippo Boncompagni, to greet the new king of France, Henry III, in the pope's name and to secure the king's support of Catholic interests in France. The Boncompagnis met the king in Venice on 18 July 1574 and accompanied him to Ferrara on 29 July. Whether Giacomo continued on to Mantua and Turin with Henry in August, or whether he left, as his cousin did, after the visit to Ferrara, is not known.[10] In any case, his mission on this trip was a glamorous one, and his return would have provided an appropriate occasion for a musical tribute to him.

The pieces in this book display a wide range of styles, from light and frivolous to relatively serious. On the basis of textual and musical characteristics, they can be divided into four categories: fourteen *canzoni alla napolitana* (nos. [2–5], [8], [10–15], [17–19]), five madrigals (nos. [1], [7], [9], [16], [20]), one dialogue (no. [6]), and one eight-voice *mascherata* (no. [21]). They are ordered in the source on the basis of voice combinations and key signatures. The six-voice pieces fall into three groups: the first (nos. [1–8]) contains pieces with the sopranos and either the tenors or the basses paired (SSATTB or SSATBB); the second (nos. [9–15]) contains pieces

with three tenors (SATTTB); and the third (nos. [16–20]) contains pieces with the altos and tenors paired (SAATTB), except in the last piece, which has three tenors. All of the pieces in the first and third groups have *cantus mollis* signatures (one flat), while those in the second group have *cantus durus* signatures (no flat). The pieces are not arranged on the basis of mode within the groups, however. Each group begins with a madrigal, and the third ends with one as well; the anonymous piece (no. [7]) is the only madrigal found in the middle of a group and may, therefore, not have been part of Ferretti's original plan. The eight-voice *mascherata*, the most showy piece in the book, concludes the collection.

The Canzoni alla napolitana

All of the *canzoni alla napolitana* are probably arrangements of earlier three-voice pieces, although models are known for only eight of them (nos. [2], [8], [11], [13–15], [17], [19]). No. [12] ("Non è dolor") is musically related to a setting of the same text in Regnart's *Primo libro delle canzone italiane a cinque voci* (Vienna: Mair, 1574), which is probably based on the same (now lost) model as Ferretti's piece. No musically related settings are known for the texts of the remaining five *canzoni alla napolitana* (nos. [3–5], [10], [18]), but their textual and musical styles are indistinguishable from those of the pieces known to be arrangements of earlier works.[11]

The known models for the above arrangements are found in the Appendix to this edition (nos. [2a], [8a], [11a], [13a-15a], [17a], [19a]). (The sources of the models are discussed below, in the section The Edition.) They are typical three-voice *canzoni alla napolitana* from popular collections of the time. They treat the subject of love in a light-hearted manner, often with stereotyped metaphors. Their vocabulary and syntax are simple and unpretentious, although rarely colored by Neapolitan dialect. Each text contains four strophes of three or four lines, the last two of which invariably rhyme. In some cases, the last line or pair of lines forms a refrain.

The music of these models is light and simple, in keeping with the nature of the texts. It is invariably strophic, usually with an internal form of *aabcc* or *aabb* within each strophe. One piece ("Bon cacciator," no. [17a]), however, has an internal form of *abcc*. The textures are predominantly homophonic, with occasional passages of light imitation, especially in the final sections. The rhythms, which are always notated in C, consist mostly of semiminims and occasional minims, which are often grouped in irregular ways to produce a lively effect. The minim is always audible as a mensural unit, so that irregular groups of semiminims are heard as deviations from a norm that is always re-established at cadences. There are, however, no regular norms for the grouping of minims, and the total number of minims in a piece may be even or odd.

The text settings in the models are almost exclusively syllabic. Repetition of partial lines of text is common. Since the *caesurae* do not always fall at corresponding points in all stanzas, these repetitions sometimes involve illogical groups of words, or even fragments of words, in stanzas other than the first (as in the last line of stanza four in "Bon cacciator," no. [17a]). Such devices contribute to the rustic effect of the genre.

A few of these pieces include features that might be interpreted as musical representations in the first strophes of the texts, but they are so mild and general that they do not make the music inappropriate for subsequent strophes. For example, the imitation at the beginning of "Bon cacciator" (no. [17a]) might represent the idea of chasing that is implicit in the subject of the hunt, and the short melisma on "rallegri" (cheers) in "O faccia che rallegri" (no. [19a]) might represent the mood of that word.

In spite of their basically popular style, these three-voice models reveal their aristocratic origin through the use of occasional quotations and paraphrases of more serious poetry and music. "Ancor che col partir" (no. [11a]) is a textual and musical parody of the madrigal "Ancor che col partire," with words by Alfonso d'Avalos and music by Cipriano de Rore.[12] "Occhi leggiadri" (no. [15a]) opens with a quotation of verse seven of Petrarch's *canzone* "Perché la vita è breve" and ends with a refrain quoted from the opening verse of a paraphrase of Bembo's madrigal "Che ti val saettarmi" (beginning with the words "Che giova saettar un che si more"). This poem had been set to music by Hubert Naich in *Il primo libro d'i madrigali de diversi eccellentissimi autori a misura di breve* (Venice: Gardane, 1542; RISM 1542[17]), and Naich's music is paraphrased in connection with the verbal quotation.[13]

Ferretti's arrangements of these models include only the first stanza of each text, but are much longer and more complex musically. The large-scale formal designs of the models are retained in most of them, but altered slightly in a few: in no. [11] ("Ancor che col partir"), the repetition of the A section is omitted, and in no. [14] ("Ognun s'allegra"), the form is changed from *aabcc* to *aabb* by combining the second and third lines of the poem in a single section. Sectional repetitions, which are always literal in the models, are usually varied with voice exchange and occasionally modified in other ways in Ferretti's arrangements. Within each section, the musical material of the model is greatly expanded and developed. Phrases or shorter musical units are repeated with different groups of voices, often on different pitch levels; motives from the model are developed in imitation; and phrases are extended through the interpolation of freely composed material. The melody of the model normally migrates among several voices of the arrangement; it remains in a single voice (the quinto) only in no. [14] ("Ognun s'allegra").

The rhythms of Ferretti's arrangements also differ significantly from those of the models, even though the rhythmic styles of their individual voices are usually identical to those of the models. By treating motives in imitation and varying the rhythms of different voices, Ferretti often produced rather elaborate rhythmic counterpoint, much more complex than the occasional conflicting rhythms among different voices of the models. He also organized his rhythms on the basis of regular semibreve, as well as minim, mensural units. All pieces end at the beginning of a semibreve unit, and final cadences of concluding repeated sections are often modified to make them do so. Repeated sections are sometimes displaced by a minim with respect to the semibreve mensural unit, but never when this procedure would result in moving a semibreve from a non-syncopated to a syncopated position or *vice versa*. Rests are also notated in such a way as to distinguish between syncopated and non-syncopated semibreves, the former always being notated as two minims.

The relationship of the music to the text in Ferretti's arrangements is essentially similar to that in the models. All representational devices and borrowings from earlier compositions are retained. In addition, Ferretti uses coloration on the first syllable of the word "sera" (evening) in no. [2] ("Dolci colli fioriti"), perhaps only to make the notation more correct—the model has an imperfect breve before another breve at that point, violating the rule of *similis ante similem semper perfecta*—but perhaps also to symbolize the meaning of the word.

The six *canzoni alla napolitana* without known models (nos. [3–5], [10], [12], [18]) are very similar to the eight arrangements of known models. All of them are based on texts with the characteristic form and style of the *canzone alla napolitana*. One (no. [5], "Ho inteso dir") employs the classical image of the dying swan, drawn from Martial's distich "Dulcia defecta"[14] and popularized in the sixteenth century by the madrigal "Il bianco e dolce cigno," with words by Alfonso d'Avalos and music by Jacob Arcadelt.[15] Their musical forms and styles are also identical to those of the known arrangements. Several of them include fairly specific representational devices: texted fusae symbolize the ideas of "fretta" (hurry) in no. [18] ("Mettetevi in battaglia") and "fuggito" (fled) in no. [4] ("Mirate che m'ha fatto"); contrary motion between paired voices symbolizes "contra" (against) in no. [18] ("Mettetevi in battaglia"); and slow motion, descending melodic lines, and suspensions symbolize "dolor" (sorrow) in no. [12] ("Non è dolor"). Whether or not these devices were found in the models for these pieces (assuming such models existed) cannot, of course, be determined, but some of them are sufficiently extreme that they were almost certainly exaggerated in the arrangements, even if they were present in the models.

The Madrigals

The five madrigals (nos. [1], [7], [9], [16], [20]) are all based on longer and more serious poems than the *canzoni alla napolitana*, although in keeping with the spirit of the collection, they are all basically cheerful in mood. The poems include one sonnet, one *ballata*, and three madrigals. The sonnet (no. [1], "Com'al primo apparir") is an anonymous dedicatory piece referring to Boncompagni's return and incorporating his name into the text. The *ballata* (no. [16], "Qual donna canterà") is a slightly corrupt version of a poem from the second *giornata* of Boccaccio's *Decameron*; in the *prima parte* (which includes the refrain and first stanza of the poem), lines 6–7 are changed from "Non de' sospir né dell'amare pene / Ch'or più dolce mi fanno il tuo diletto" to "Non dell'amate pene, / Né di sospiri," and different individual words are substituted for the original ones at several points throughout the poem. Ferretti labeled his setting of this piece "*canzona*," apparently because of the strophic form of the text, which was often associated with the poetic form of the Petrarchan *canzone*, and therefore with multipartite madrigals in general, in the sixteenth century. The corruptions in the version of the text that he set suggest that he may not have understood the poetic form.[16] The poems in madrigal form are all anonymous. No. [9] ("Nasce la gioia mia") is a parody of the anonymous poem "Nasce la pena mia," which was set to music by many composers of the period.

The musical styles of the madrigals are somewhat more complex and serious than those of the *canzoni alla napolitana*. Their forms are less distinctly sectional, since phrases are overlapped more often and for longer durations, and opening sections are never repeated, although closing sections are, in some cases. The madrigals by Ferretti are invariably notated in ¢ and have more varied rhythms and

greater contrasts in rate of motion than his *canzoni alla napolitana*. The anonymous madrigal (no. [7], "Ecco ch'io lass'il core") is in ¢, but is otherwise similar to Ferretti's madrigals. No. [9] ("Nasce la gioia mia") parodies the music of Alessandro Striggio's setting of "Nasce la pena mia."[17]

Musical representation is more frequent and more extreme in the madrigals than in the *canzoni alla napolitana*. Words associated with happiness are regularly set with fast rhythmic figures, often including fusae, and are sometimes ornamented with short melismas, while words associated with sorrow or calm are set with longer note values, sometimes combined with descending motion or flatted notes. More specific meanings are also symbolized musically in many places. For example, in no. [1] ("Com'al primo apparir"), the word "cantar" (sing) is associated with a melisma, and the echoing of the name "Boncompagno" is illustrated with echo effects in the music; in nos. [9] ("Nasce la gioia mia") and [16] ("Qual donna canterà"), the word "sol" is associated with the notes corresponding to the solmization syllable "sol."

The Dialogue

The dialogue (no. [6], "Su, su, su, non più dormir") is an unusual piece differing in character from both the madrigals and the *canzoni alla napolitana*.[18] Its text is simple prose, lacking in literary quality of any kind, and its content is blatantly obscene. Ferretti treated it humorously, setting the opening line in a serious, contrapuntal style, and then changing suddenly to simple, declamatory homophony with contrasting voice groups representing the two speakers in the second, third, and fourth lines. The final line is in a somewhat more madrigalesque style, but lighter, faster, and more homophonic than the opening one.

The Mascherata

The eight-voice *mascherata* (no. [21], "O consiacaldari!"), which is labeled as such in the source, is a quasi-dramatic representation of a market scene. Most of the singers represent venders hawking their wares: a tinsmith, a chimneysweep, a chestnut salesman, and a merchant of unspecified wares for beautiful women. One singer, possibly a shopper or a passer-by, sings the famous folksong "La bella Franceschina."[19] The texts of the vendors are in prose, and are probably imitations of actual market cries. The tinsmith and the merchant sing in Venetian dialect, and the chestnut salesman sings in the dialect of the Marches. The cry of the tinsmith can also be found in a *villotta* by Filippo Azzaiolo,[20] and that of the chestnut salesman in a *canzone* by

Jacques du Pont.[21] In both of these pieces, the words and musical themes of the street cries are the same as those in Ferretti's *mascherata*. Ferretti probably took the themes from these earlier musical compositions, rather than from street cries directly.

Ferretti's *mascherata* bears little resemblance to earlier compositions in that genre, most of which were for three or four voices and in the same poetic and musical style as the *canzone alla napolitana*. Because of its combination of several independent texts and melodies, including at least three pre-existent popular tunes (the two market cries and the folksong), Ferretti's *mascherata* is more closely related to the quodlibet than to the earlier *mascherata*. It is, however, an unusual piece, not following the conventions of any single, established genre. It may have served as a model for pieces based on London street cries by Thomas Weelkes, Orlando Gibbons, and Richard Dering.[22]

Performance

Ferretti's *canzoni* were composed for a vocal ensemble with one singer on each part. Although a group of this type is the best performance medium for them, the style of the music is such that it would not be inappropriate for a small choral ensemble. Instruments could also be used to double the vocal parts, provided they did not interfere with the clarity of the texts or the musical textures.

The three-voice *canzoni alla napolitana* in the Appendix may also be performed by an ensemble of vocal soloists, although in the sixteenth century they were more often performed by a soloist with an instrumental accompaniment played on a lute or harpsichord.[23] This medium emphasizes the predominant role of the top voice in the texture and allows the singer the maximum flexibility in interpreting the music.

The Edition

This edition is based on the first edition of Ferretti's *Secondo libro delle canzoni a sei voci* (Venice: Heirs of Girolamo Scotto, 1575). All pieces in the source are included, in their original order. A separate discussion follows on the sources and editorial policies for the pieces in the Appendix.

The work was published in six partbooks, labeled Canto, Alto, Tenore, Basso, Quinto, and Sesto. (In the eight-voice *mascherata*, the voices labeled "[Canto II]" and "[Tenore III]" are found in the Quinto partbook, and those labeled "[Canto III]" and "[Tenore II]" are found in the Sesto partbook.)

Two complete and three incomplete copies of the set are extant.[24] It was reprinted in 1579, 1581, and 1586, probably in all cases by the Scotto firm, which published all extant editions of Ferretti's works.[25] The publisher of the 1581 edition cannot be established with certainty, however, since the only known copy of it was destroyed during World War II. Five pieces from the collection were included in north-European anthologies: nos. [4] and [8] in *Symphonia angelica* (Antwerp: Phalèse and Bellère, 1585),[26] nos. [6] and [7] in *Musica divina* (Antwerp: Phalèse and Bellère, 1583),[27] and no. [9] in *Harmonia celeste* (Antwerp: Phalèse and Bellère, 1583).[28] All extant editions of the complete book and of the individual pieces from it are based directly or indirectly on the first edition and do not differ from it in any significant ways. Most errors, except the most obvious ones such as incorrect clefs, key signatures, and mensuration signs, are duplicated in all later editions. These editions therefore have no independent value in establishing the correct versions of the pieces; additional errors in them are therefore not mentioned in the following discussion.

The voice designations, clefs, key signatures, mensuration signs, and initial notes are shown at the beginning of each piece. Errors in the incipits are not corrected, although they are corrected in the transcriptions.

The treble clef is used in this edition for all voices originally notated in soprano or alto clefs, the transposing treble clef for voices in tenor clef, and the bass clef for voices in bass clef. In a few pieces, voices in alto clef go as low as d. These parts are nevertheless transcribed in treble clef, rather than transposing treble clef, because they are probably more appropriate for altos than for tenors. Their general tessituras are higher than those of parts notated in tenor clef, and one of them goes as high as b'-flat. Since there was no absolute standard of pitch in the sixteenth century, any piece may be transposed in performance to a pitch level appropriate to the available voices.

In all pieces or sections of pieces in binary mensurations, the note values in the edition are the same as those in the source, except that final longs are replaced by the values necessary to complete the final measures of pieces. The music is barred in breve units when the original mensuration is ₵ and in semibreve units when it is C, to retain the distinction that Ferretti makes between these two mensurations. The pieces in ₵ generally have a higher percentage of "white notes" (breves, semibreves, and minims) than those in C, although the same range of written values is found in both mensurations. In repeated sections, the music is sometimes displaced by a semibreve with respect to the tactus in ₵, or by a minim in C, but never by a minim in ₵. The signature ₵ might imply a slightly faster tempo than C, but the difference between them cannot be very great.

The notation of ternary rhythm in the source is inconsistent. In nos. [1] and [2], the signature is Ø 3, and the breves are perfect; in no. [6], the signature is 3, and the semibreves are perfect; and in no. [16], the ternary rhythm is notated with coloration only, without a change of signature, and the colored semibreves are in groups of three. In all cases, one ternary measure (a perfect breve in nos. [1] and [2], a perfect semibreve in no. [6], and three colored semibreves in no. [16]) is equivalent to one semibreve of the preceding and following duple passages. The note values in this edition are therefore reduced by half in the ternary passages of nos. [1], [2], and [16], but are not reduced in no. [6].

In this edition, accidentals are placed beside the notes if they are found in the source and above them if they are supplied by the editor. Repetitions of accidentals that are redundant in modern notation are omitted, but cautionary accidentals in the source that were used to prevent performers from applying rules of *musica ficta* are included. No cautionary accidentals have been added by the editor.

Solid brackets (⌐⌐) indicate ligatures in the source, and open brackets (⌐ ¬) indicate coloration.

Sections of music that are repeated literally are always written out in full in the source. In order to save space, repeat signs are used wherever possible in this edition. In many cases, however, exchanges of parts by two paired voices or other minor deviations of the second statement of a section from the first make the use of repeat signs impossible.

In the texts, spellings are modernized, except where that procedure would significantly affect the pronunciation of words. The following changes were made to make spellings conform to modern practice: (a) accent marks were added or removed (e.g., *cosi/così; và/va*); (b) single consonants were doubled or double consonants made single (e.g. *matina/mattina, ruggiadosi/rugiadosi*); (c) separate words were combined into single words (e.g., *per che/perché, ogn'un/ognun*); (d) silent h's were removed (e.g., *hor/or*); (e) letters were changed if the change produced no effect or only a minor effect on pronunciation (e.g., *gratia/grazia, inpaccio/impaccio, giovenetto/giovanetto, et/ed*). Original spellings were not changed, however, if such changes would significantly affect pronunciation (e.g., *voi/vuoi, core/cuore, moro/muoio*). In some cases, final letters of words were replaced by apostrophes, and in other cases, final letters (replaced by apostrophes in the source) were added to clarify the pronunciation. Punctuation is editorially supplied. Capitalization is used for the beginnings of all poetic lines, as it usually is in the source, and for all other words capitalized in the source. Text repetitions indicated by the symbol *ij* in the source are not distinguished in the edition, since this symbol poses no ambiguities with respect to interpretation.

In the source, two pieces (nos. [16] and [21]) have labels suggesting the genres to which they belong. These labels are included here at the beginnings of the scores.

In general, the versions of the pieces found in the source are quite accurate. The minor errors in the following list have been corrected in this edition on the basis of the musical or poetic context. Pitch designation follows the Helmholtz system in which middle C is c'.

No. [1]: M. 1, Canto, mensuration is C.

No. [3]: M. 1, Basso, flat is in the first space.

No. [4]: M. 1, Quinto, mensuration is ₵. M. 20, Alto, note is a fusa. M. 21, Alto, notes 1 through 3 are fusae and note 4 is a semiminim.

No. [6]: M. 1, Basso, flat is in the first space.

No. [7]: M. 42, Quinto, note 1 is f-sharp. M. 70, Quinto, note 1 is a.

No. [11]: M. 61, Alto, note 1 is f'-sharp—editorially emended by analogy with m. 30.

No. [12]: M. 1, Canto, note 1 is f'.

No. [17]: Text, last word is "vivo" instead of "viva."

No. [19]: Text, word is "rallegra" instead of "rallegri."

No. [20]: Canto, clef on the first staff is mezzo-soprano.

THE APPENDIX

The sources of the pieces in the Appendix of this edition are as follows:

No. [2a]: Francesco de Laudis, *Dolci colli fioriti*: Giulio Bonagiunta, *Il primo libro de canzon napolitane a tre voci, con due alla venetiana* (Venice: Scotto, 1565).[29]

No. [8a]: [Anonymous], *Occhi, non occhi*: Giulio Bonagiunta, *Canzone napolitane a tre voci, Secondo libro* (Venice: Scotto, 1566).[30]

No. [11a]: Gasparo Fiorino, *Ancor che col partir*: Gasparo Fiorino, *La nobilità di Roma* (Venice: Scotto, 1571).[31]

No. [13a]: Marc'Antonio Mazzone, *O saporito volto: Corona delle napolitane a tre et a quattro voci* (Venice: Scotto, 1570).[32]

No. [14a]: Marc'Antonio Mazzone, *Ognun s'allegra: Corona delle napolitane a tre et a quattro voci* (Venice: Scotto, 1570).

No. [15a]: [Anonymous], *Occhi leggiadri: Il primo libro delle villotte alla napolitana . . . a tre voci* (Venice: Gardano, 1560).[33]

No. [17a]: [Anonymous], *Bon cacciator: Corona delle napolitane a tre et a quattro voci* (Venice: Scotto, 1570).[34]

No. [19a]: [Anonymous], *O faccia che rallegri: Il terzo libro delle villotte alla napolitana . . . a tre voci* (Venice: Gardano, 1560).[35]

Whenever possible, the scores in this edition are based on the first published editions of these pieces. Since the first editions of nos. [15a] and [19a] are incomplete, however, this edition is based on later sources of them (RISM 1571[5] for no. [15a] and RISM 1567[17] for no. [19a]). Only one source has been consulted for each piece.

The upper two voices of these pieces are always transcribed in treble clef; the lowest voice is transcribed in bass clef when the original clef was tenor and in transposing treble clef when it was alto.

The original mensuration in all of these pieces is ₵. Since their rhythmic style does not depend on regular semibreve units, however, the barring in the edition is irregular. Unless otherwise indicated, all note values remain equivalent when the meter changes.

The note values in the editions of these pieces are the same as those in the sources, except mm. 6–10 of no. [2a], which were originally notated with the proportional signature 3, with three semibreves per measure. In this passage, the note values in the edition are halved.

Repeated sections are notated in this edition with repeat signs. In the sources, such sections are written out in nos. [13a], [14a], and [17a].

All other editorial policies are the same for these pieces as for those of Ferretti.

The following errors in the sources of these pieces have been corrected on the basis of the musical or poetic context:

No. [8a]: M. 4, Tenore, note 2 is c''.

No. [14a]: M. 2, Basso, last note is d' the first time, but e' in the written-out repetition.

No. [17a]: Last word of text of refrain is "vivo" instead of "viva."

No. [19a]: Stanza 1, line 2, Canto and Basso, word 4 is "illustre" instead of "illustrate." M. 5, Tenore, note 1 is a semiminim.

Acknowledgments

I am grateful to the Bayerische Staatsbibliothek of Munich for supplying me with a microfilm of the first edition of Ferretti's *Secondo libro delle canzoni a sei voci* and giving me permission to prepare an edition of it. I would also like to thank Nino Pirrotta and Kristin Murtaugh for their assistance with the editing of the texts.

Ruth I. DeFord
April 1983   Hastings-on-Hudson, New York

Notes

1. Ferretti's position at the Cathedral of Ancona is documented on the title page of his second book of *canzoni a 6* (1575). His positions at Santa Casa in Loreto are discussed in Giovanni Tebaldini, *L'Archivio musicale della Cappella Lauretana* (Loreto, 1921), p. 29, and in Floriano Grimaldi, *La cappella musicale di Loreto nel Cinquecento: note d'archivio* (Loreto, 1981), pp. 56–57. Ferretti's positions at Gemona and Cividale del Friuli are mentioned by Iain Fenlon in *The New Grove Dictionary of Music and Musicians* (s.v. "Ferretti, Giovanni") and are probably documented in Giuseppe Vale, *La schola cantorum di Gemona e i suoi maestri* (Gemona, 1908), which was unavailable to this editor. Fenlon claims that Ferretti held the position in Ancona until 1579, but the only evidence for this claim is the fact that his title "Maestro di Capella del Duomo di Ancona" is found on the title page of the 1579 reprint of his second book of *canzoni a 6*. Since, however, the same title is also repeated in the reprint of 1586, when he is known to have been working elsewhere, the evidence that he was still in Ancona in 1579 is very weak.

2. The first editions of these books are as follows: *Canzone alla napolitana a cinque voci* (Venice: Scotto, 1567); *Il secondo libro delle canzoni alla napolitana a cinque voci* (Venice: Scotto, 1569); *Il terzo libro delle napolitane a cinque voci* (Venice: Scotto, 1570); *Il quarto libro delle napolitane a cinque voci* (Venice: Scotto, 1571); *Il primo libro delle canzoni alla napolitana a sei voci* (Venice: Scotto, 1573); *Il secondo libro delle canzoni a sei voci* (Venice: Scotto, 1575); and *Il quinto libro delle canzoni alla napolitana a cinque voci* (Venice: Scotto, 1585).

3. The anthologies including his *canzoni* are as follows: *Harmonia celeste* (Antwerp: Phalèse and Bellère, 1583; RISM 1583[14]), *Musica divina* (Antwerp: Phalèse and Bellère, 1583; RISM 1583[15]), *Symphonia angelica* (Antwerp: Phalèse and Bellère, 1585; RISM 1585[19]), *Musica transalpina* (London: East, 1588; RISM 1588[29]), *Liber secundus Gemmae musicalis* (Nuremberg: Gerlach, 1589; RISM 1589[8]), and all subsequent editions of these works. Facsimile editions of RISM 1583[15], 1583[14], and 1585[19] are in *Corpus of Early Music in Facsimile*, ed. B. Huys (Brussels, 1970–), vols. 19–21.

4. See Donna G. Cardamone, *The canzone villanesca alla napolitana and Related Forms, 1537–1570*, 2 vols., Studies in Musicology, no. 45 (Ann Arbor, 1981), 1:67–92, and Donna G. Cardamone, "Forme musicali e metriche della canzone villanesca e della villanella alla napolitana," *Rivista italiana di musicologia* XII (1977): 25–72, for detailed studies of text forms in the *canzone alla napolitana*. All of Willaert's *canzone* arrangements are found in *Adrian Willaert and His Circle: Canzone villanesche alla napolitana and villotte*, ed. Donna G. Cardamone, Recent Researches in the Music of the Renaissance, vol. XXX (Madison, Wisconsin: A-R Editions, 1979).

5. See Cardamone, *The canzone villanesca*, 1:179–208, for a study of the music arrangements of *canzoni alla napolitana* in the period immediately preceding that of Ferretti's works.

6. Iain Fenlon's statement in *The New Grove Dictionary* that Ferretti's texts are hardly ever derived from popular sources is incorrect. More than half of them are found in earlier collections of *canzoni alla napolitana*.

7. See Alfred Einstein, *The Italian Madrigal*, 3 vols. (Princeton, 1949), 2:595–596, for an example of a *canzone* from Ferretti's second book *a 5* in which the text painting in the first stanza makes the use of the same music for the remaining stanzas impossible.

8. Ludwig Freiherr von Pastor, *Geschichte der Päpste*, vol. 9 (Freiburg, 1923), pp. 23–24.

9. This relationship does not, therefore, indicate that Ferretti had connections with Rome in the 1570s, as Fenlon suggests in *The New Grove Dictionary*. It is possible, however, that his later Roman contacts may have been made through Boncompagni.

10. This trip is discussed in Pastor, *Geschichte der Päpste*, 9:381–382, and in Pier[re] de Nolhac and Angelo Solerti, *Il viaggio in Italia di Enrico III, Re di Francia* (Rome, 1890), p. 259.

11. Other settings are known for the texts of nos. [5] and [10], but they are musically unrelated to Ferretti's pieces. Catterino Bianchi's "Ho inteso a dir," in his *Primo libro delle canzonette a cinque voci* (Venice: Amadino, 1588), is based on the text of no. [5], and Giovanni Giacomo Gastoldi's "Un nuovo cacciator," in his *Canzoni a cinque voci . . . libro primo* (Venice: Gardano, 1581), is based on the text of no. [10].

12. Modern edition in Cipriano de Rore, *Opera omnia*, ed. B. Meier, Corpus mensurabilis musicae, ([Rome], 1959–77), 14/4:31–32.

13. The complex history of this refrain as a textual and musical quotation is discussed in Cardamone, *The canzone villanesca*, 1:216–222.

14. No. 77 from Book XIII of his *Epigrammata*. Modern edition in Martial, *Epigrams*, ed. Walter C. A. Ker, 2 vols., Loeb Classical Library (Cambridge, Mass., 1968), 2:418.

15. Modern edition in Jacob Arcadelt, *Opera omnia*, ed. A. Seay, Corpus mensurabilis musicae, ([Rome], 1965–70), 31/2:38–40.

16. Modern edition of the original poem in Giovanni Boccaccio, *Tutte le opere*, ed. Vittore Branca, vol. 4 (Milan, 1976), p. 230. The same corrupt version of the poem was set to music by Girolamo Scotto in his *Madrigali a tre voci* (Venice: Scotto, 1570), but Ferretti's piece is not related musically to Scotto's.

17. Modern edition in Philippe de Monte, *Complete Works*, ed. C. Van den Borren and J. Van Nuffel (Düsseldorf, 1927–39), Appendix, pp. 1–10.

18. This piece is published in Johannes Hol, *Horatio Vecchi's weltliche Werke* (Strassburg, 1934), Appendix, pp. 4–9.

19. For a history of the text and music of this folksong, see Warren Kirkendale, "Franceschina, Girometta, and their Companions in a Madrigal *a diversi linguaggi* by Luca Marenzio and Orazio Vecchi," *Acta musicologica* XLIV (1972): 188–194. Ferretti's piece should be added to Kirkendale's list of sources of the song, p. 189.

20. Azzaiolo's *villotta*, "O spazzacamin," is found in his first book of *Villotte del fiore* (Venice: Gardano, 1557; RISM 1557[18]). A modern edition is found in Filippo Azzaiolo, *Villotte del fiore*, ed. F. Vatielli (Bologna, 1921), pp. 15–16. A madrigal by Francesco Bifetto beginning with the words "O spazzacamin," from his *Secondo libro di madrigali a quatro voci* (Venice: Gardane, 1548), is not related musically to the pieces by Azzaiolo and Ferretti.

21. Du Pont's *canzone*, "Cald'arost," is found in *Il vero terzo libro di madrigali de diversi autori a note negre, composti da eccellentissimi musici, con la canzon di cald'arost . . . a quatro voci* (Venice: Gardane, 1549; RISM 1549[31]). For a discussion and a modern edition of this piece, see Alberto Cametti, "Jacques du Pont e la sua 'Canzon di cald'arost,' " *Rivista musicale italiana* XXIII (1916): 273–288. I am grateful to Martin Morell for calling my attention to this piece.

22. Modern editions of these pieces, plus one by an anonymous composer, are in *Consort Songs*, ed. P. Brett, Musica Brittanica, vol. 22, 2nd ed. (London, 1974), pp. 102–147.

23. See Cardamone, *The canzone villanesca*, 1:223, for evidence concerning the performance practice of the *canzone alla napolitana*.

24. The complete sets are in the Bayerische Staatsbibliothek in Munich and the Biblioteca Nazionale in Turin. The incomplete sets are in the Civico Museo Bibliografico Musicale in Bologna, the Archivio del Duomo in Ancona, and the Biblioteca Riccardiana in Florence. This edition is based on the set in the Bayerische Staatsbibliothek.

25. The 1581 edition is not listed in RISM, but is listed in Emil Vogel et al., *Bibliografia della musica italiana vocale profana pubblicata dal 1500 al 1700*, 3 vols. ([Pomezia], 1977), 1:629.

26. RISM 1585[19], reprinted in RISM 1590[17], 1594[8], 1611[12], and 1629[8]. Facsimile of the first edition in *Corpus of Early Music in Facsimile*, ed. B. Huys (Brussels, 1970–), vol. 21.

27. RISM 1583[15], reprinted in RISM 1588[16], 1591[11], 1595[4], 1606[7], 1614[13], 1623[7], and 1634[6]. Facsimile of the first edition in *Corpus of Early Music in Facsimile*, ed. B. Huys (Brussels, 1970–), vol. 19.

28. RISM 1583[14], reprinted in RISM 1589[9], 1593[4], 1605[8], 1614[12], and 1628[14]. Facsimile of the first edition in *Corpus of Early Music in Facsimile*, ed. B. Huys (Brussels, 1970–), vol. 20.

29. RISM 1565[12], reprinted in RISM 1567[18].

30. RISM 1566[7].

31. RISM 1571[8], reprinted in RISM 1573[19].

32. RISM 1570[18], reprinted in RISM 1572[5].

33. RISM 1560[12], reprinted in RISM 1562[11], 1565[11], and 1571[5].

34. RISM 1570[18], reprinted in RISM 1572[5]. The music of this piece is not the same as that of Giovanni Zappasorgo's setting of the same text in his *Secondo libro delle napolitane a tre voci* (Venice: Scotto, 1576), as Alfred Einstein suggests in his Appendix to Emil Vogel, *Bibliothek der gedruckten weltlichen Vokalmusik Italiens aus den Jahren 1500–1700*, rev. and enlarged by A. Einstein (Hildesheim, 1962), 2:680, first published in *Notes* III (1945–46): 271.

35. RISM 1560[14], reprinted in RISM 1562[13], 1565[11], and 1567[17].

Texts and Translations

All translations have been done by the editor.

[1] Com'al primo apparir

Com'al primo apparir del chiaro giorno
S'allegra il Ciel, ride la terra, e fuori
Corron più chiare l'acque, i suoi colori
Spiega la bella Flora d'ogn'intorno,
Cantan gli augei l'aspettato ritorno
Della dolce alba, e i rugiadosi fiori
Spirano in ogni part'Arabi odori,
Rendendo il proprio suol ricco ed adorno,

SECONDA PARTE

Così al vostro tornar le vostre genti
Mostrar gioia, signor, estrem'e vera:
Sendo seren'il ciel, placid'i venti,
Cantar le sacre ninfe, e ogni riviera
Risonò "Buoncompagno" in dolci accenti,
E tornò vaga e nova primavera.

(As at the first appearance of a clear day Heaven rejoices, the earth laughs, and the waters run clearer, beautiful Flora spreads her colors all around, the birds sing the expected return of the sweet dawn, and the dew-covered flowers everywhere breathe Arabian odors, making the ground itself rich and adorned,

Even so at your return, Sir, your people showed extreme and true joy: the sky being serene and the winds gentle, the sacred nymphs sang, and every shore echoed "Buoncompagno" in sweet accents, and spring returned, new and lovely.)

[2, 2a] Dolci colli fioriti

Dolci colli fiorit', a me sì cari,
Che vedet'il mio sol mattin'e sera,
Deh fatemi un favore:
Diteli che mi moro di dolore.

Poiché quei raggi suoi sono sì chiari,
Perché nel giorno a me mandan la sera?
Deh fatemi un favore:
Diteli che mi moro di dolore.

Se saranno ver me cotanto avari,
Saranno ancor cagion che presto io pera.
Deh fatemi un favore:
Diteli che mi moro di dolore.

Per acquetar gli ardenti miei sospiri,
Dicovi la cagion di miei martiri.
Deh fatemi un favore:
Diteli che mi moro di dolore.

(Sweet, flowery hills, so dear to me, who see my sun morning and evening, do me a favor: tell her that I am dying of sorrow.

Since her rays are so bright, why do they send evening to me in the daytime? Do me a favor: tell her that I am dying of sorrow.

If they are so stingy toward me, they will soon cause me to die. Do me a favor: tell her that I am dying of sorrow.

To quiet my ardent sighs, I am telling you the cause of my sufferings. Do me a favor: tell her that I am dying of sorrow.)

[3] Voi che te dica

Voi che te dica il vero a buona cera?
Che non ha troppo ch'io me n'adonai
Ch'hai pochi fatti, ma parole assai.

(Do you want me to tell you the truth with a cheerful face? It has not been too long that I have been aware that your actions are few, but your words too many.)

[4] Mirate che m'ha fatto

Mirate che m'ha fatto sto mio core,
Che s'è fuggito per seguir mia diva,
E mormorando va di riv'in riva.

(See what my heart has done to me: it has fled to follow my goddess, and goes murmuring from shore to shore.)

[5] Ho inteso dir

Ho inteso dir da molti che lo sanno
Ch'il cigno mor cantando.
O fortunat'uccel, or poi ben dire
Che vita t'è 'l morire.

(I have heard it said by many who know that the swan dies singing. O fortunate bird, now you can say that dying is life to you.)

[6] Su, su, su, non più dormir

Su, su, su, non più dormir, ché la notte se ne va!
Deh dimmi, cor mio bel, che voi?
Non dormir più, ch'io te'l dirò!
Stringimi ben ch'io moro, dolce vita mia.
Ahimè, non più, ché tu mi fai morire!

(Up, up, up, don't sleep anymore, for the night is flying!
Tell me, my sweetheart, what do you want?
Don't sleep anymore, and I will tell you.
Squeeze me tightly, so that I die, my sweetheart.
Ah, no more, you are making me die.)

[7] Ecco ch'io lass'il core

Ecco ch'io lass'il core
A chi nutrisce il suo del mio dolore.
Deh come vivrò io
Lungi d'ogni ben mio?
Dunque morrommi, e perché chi m'annoia
Viva della mia mort'in maggior gioia.

(Here I give my heart to one who feeds hers on my sorrow. Alas, how will I live far from my treasure? Therefore I will die, so that the one who tortures me can live in greater joy because of my death.)

[8, 8a] Occhi, non occhi

Occhi, non occhi, ma lucente stelle
Sono i tuoi occhi, ch'agli amant'il core
Con sguardi leghi nel laccio d'amore.

Non sono labbra quesse labbra belle;
Son gioie e perle, e di corall'il core,
Che or vita, or morte, dona a tutte l'ore.

Non furo al mondo sì belle mammelle,
Che a noi stillasse sì dolce liquore,
Che per gustar'al mondo non si more.

Quess'occhi foron ch'allaccio d'amore
Al primo sguardo mi legar'il core,
Che vive in morte, e nella vita more.

(Eyes, your eyes are not eyes, but shining stars that bind with glances the hearts of lovers in the bond of love.

Those beautiful lips are not lips; they are jewels and pearls, and your heart is coral, which gives now life, now death, all the time.

Never in the world were there such beautiful breasts that dripped such sweet liquid to us; one who tastes it in this world will never die.

These eyes were bonds of love which at the first glance bound my heart, which lives in death and dies in life.)

[9] Nasce la gioia mia

Nasce la gioia mia
Ogni volta ch'io mir'il mio bel sole,
E la mia vit'è ria
Qualor nol miro, perch'il sguard'è tale
Ch'ogni volta beato farmi suole.
O sol, alm'immortale,
Non t'asconder mai più, ché certo veggio,
S'io non ti miro, io non poss'aver peggio.

(My joy is born every time I see my beautiful sun, and my life is bitter whenever I do not see it, for its glance is such that it makes me blessed every time. O sun, immortal soul, do not hide yourself ever again, for I see for certain that if I do not see you, I could have nothing worse.)

[10] Un nuovo cacciator

Un nuovo cacciator segue una fera
Troppo con frett', e non la puol pigliare.
Novello cacciator, sai che voi fare?
Vatte con dio, ché tu non sai cacciare.

(A young hunter chases his prey in too much haste, and cannot catch it. New hunter, do you know what you want to do? Go away, for you do not know how to hunt.)

[11, 11a] Ancor che col partir

Ancor che col partir l'alma si mora,
Pensando di tornar, partir vorrei,
Tanto son dolci gli ritorni miei.

Perché se nel partir l'alma s'accora,
Non sente nel tornar gravosi omei,
Tanto son dolci gli ritorni miei.

E se giungo partendo all'ultim'ora,
Mi pone il ritornar vivo fra i Dei,
Tanto son dolci gli ritorni miei.

Così sento la morte e vita quando
Da voi mi parto e poi faccio ritorno,
Sol contemplando quesso viso adorno.

(Even though in parting my soul dies, when I think of returning, I want to part, since my returns are so sweet.

Because if in parting my soul is grieved, in returning it feels no painful woes, since my returns are so sweet.

And if in parting I reach my last hour, returning places me living among the gods, since my returns are so sweet.

Thus I feel death and life when I part from you and then return, just contemplating your gorgeous face.)

[12] Non è dolor

Non è dolor ch'avanzi la mia doglia,
E par che mia fortuna così voglia.
Son disperato, e pur mi segue amore,
Per consumarmi con maggior dolore.

(There is no sorrow that exceeds my sorrow, and it seems that my fortune wants it so. I am desperate, and yet love pursues me, to burn me with greater pain.)

[13, 13a] O saporito volto

O saporito volto,
Per te son fatto stolto.
Sciogli, ti prego, il laccio:
Dammi la libertà; non vo' più impaccio.

O bianca e bella mano,
Per te son fatto insano.
Or sciogli le catene:
Dammi la libertà; non vo' più pene.

O delicato aspetto,
Ho perso l'intelletto.
Dammi la libertade,
Poiché sei bella, e mostri crudeltade.

S'io vedo sciolto il laccio,
Sarò fuora d'impaccio.
S'io scioglio le catene,
Vivo contento, e poi beato mene.

(O delicious face, for you I have become crazy. Release, I beg you, the bond: give me liberty; I want no more trouble.

O white and lovely hand, for you I have gone mad. Now release the chains: give me liberty; I want no more pains.

O delicate face, I have lost my mind. Give me liberty, because you are beautiful and show me cruelty.

If I see the bond broken, I will be out of trouble. If I release the chains, I will live content and blessed.)

[14, 14a] Ognun s'allegra

Ognun s'allegra e viv'in fest'e in gioco;
S'allegra il ciel, la terra, ed ogni fiore,
Quand'esci, o chiaro sol, col tuo splendore.

Bellezza e leggiadria in ogni loco
Si vede, e par che là ci regna amore,
Quand'esci, o chiaro sol, col tuo splendore.

Ognun che viv'in amoroso foco
Si sent'allevïar ogni dolore,
Quand'esci, o chiaro sol, col tuo splendore.

Ed io, che per te vivo in gran martire,
Subito mi si rasserena il core,
Quand'esci, o chiaro sol, col tuo splendore.

(Everyone rejoices and makes merry; the sky, the earth, and every flower rejoice when you come out, o bright sun, in your splendor.

Beauty and loveliness are seen everywhere, and it seems that love reigns there, when you come out, o bright sun, in your splendor.

Everyone who lives in amorous fire feels all of his pains relieved when you come out, o bright sun, in your splendor.

And I, who live for you in great suffering, feel my heart suddenly brightened when you come out, o bright sun, in your splendor.)

[15, 15a] Occhi leggiadri

Occhi leggiadri, dov'amor fa nido,
Ché tanti strali ad impiagarmi il core?
Che giova saettar un che si more?

Moro mi di dolor, piangendo rido,
Ma di mia mort' ovunque reign' amore
Non te ne può venir largo onore.

Onor sarebb' a te, crudel infido,
S'è ver ch'hai fra li Dei forz'e valore,
Temprar'in part'il mio profund'ardore,

Non con dui occh'il cuor sempre impiagarme.
Vita non ho con che possa aitarme.
Vedi ch'io moro omai; che puoi tu farme?

(Pretty eyes, where love makes his nest, why do you send so many arrows to wound my heart? What is the use of shooting one who is dying?

I die of sorrow, I laugh weeping, but wherever love reigns, you cannot receive great honor from my death.

It would be honorable for you, cruel, faithless Love, if it is true that you have power among the gods, to temper somewhat my profound ardor,

Not constantly to wound my heart with two eyes. I have no life with which to help myself. See, I am dying now; what can you do for me?)

[16] Qual donna canterà   (Boccaccio)

Qual donna canterà, se non cant'io,
Che son contenta d'ogni mio desio?
Vien dunque, Amor, cagion d'ogni mio bene,
D'ogni speranz'e d'ogni lieto effetto;
Cantiam insieme un poco,
Non dell'amate pene,
Né di sospiri,
Ma sol del chiaro foco,

Nel qual ardendo viv'in fest'e in gioco,
Te laudando come mio signore.

SECONDA PARTE

Tu mi ponest'innanzi agli occhi, Amore,
Il primo dì ch'io nel tuo foco entrai,
Un giovanetto tale,
Che di beltà, d'ardir, e di valore
Non se ne troverebbe un maggior mai,
Né pur a lui uguale:
Di lui m'accesi tanto, che uguale
Lieta ne canto teco, signor mio.

TERZA PARTE

E quel ch'in questo m'è sommo piacere
È ch'io li piaccio quant'egli a me piace,
Amor, la tua mercede;
Per che in questo mond'il mio volere
Posseggio, e spero nell'altr'aver pace
Per quell'integra fede
Ch'io li porto. Iddio, che questo vede,
Del regno suo ancor ne sarà pio.

(What woman will sing if I do not, since I am content with all that I desire? Come therefore, Love, cause of all my joy, of every hope and every happy feeling; let us sing together a little, not of my beloved pains, nor of sighs, but only of the bright fire in which I live, burning in joy, praising you as my lord.

You put before my eyes, Love, the first day that I entered into your fire, a youth so full of beauty, courage, and valor that one could never find one better, or even equal to him. I burned for him so much that I sing happily of him with you, my lord.

And what gives me the greatest pleasure is that he likes me as much as I like him, thanks to you, Love. Because of this I have what I want in this world, and I hope in the next to have peace for that total faith that I have toward him. God, who sees this, will be generous [to me] also in his kingdom.)

[17, 17a] Bon cacciator

Bon cacciator giammai non perse caccia.
Lo cane che la seguita l'arriva;
Però voglio seguir perfin che viva.

L'agresta con lo tempo fa guarnaccia.
Pian piano s'ammaturano l'olive;
Però voglio seguir perfin che viva.

Press'al mal tempo viene la bonaccia.
Da uno sdegno grand'amor deriva;
Però voglio seguir perfin che viva.

Non vale per combatter una maglia,
E fuggir sempre incontr'alla battaglia,
Ch'al fin la donna vole della quaglia.

(A good hunter never lost a catch. The dog that chases it gets it; therefore I want to chase as long as I live.

The juice of sour grapes in time produces good wine. Gradually the olives mature; therefore I want to chase as long as I live.

After bad weather comes the calm. From indignation great love derives; therefore I want to chase as long as I live.

A coat of mail does not help in fighting, nor always fleeing in the face of battle, because in the end the woman wants some of the quail.)

[18] Mettetevi in battaglia

Mettetevi in battaglia, o pensier miei,
E contr'amor andate tutt'in fretta,
Ch'in poco spazio ne farò vendetta.

(Enter the battle, o my thoughts, and move against love in haste, for in a short time I will get revenge on him.)

[19, 19a] O faccia che rallegri

O faccia che rallegr'il paradiso,
O occhi ch'illustrate la mia vita,
Porgetimi di grazia qualche aita.

O treccie bionde e ben compiuto viso,
O gran beltade rara ed infinita,
Porgetimi di grazia qualche aita.

O viso angelicato, o dolce riso,
O bocca inzuccherata e saporita,
Porgetimi di grazia qualche aita.

Vi prego mi porgeti qualche aita,
Acciò possa anco dir, che questa vita,
L'abbia sola da voi, beltà infinita.

(O face that cheers paradise, o eyes that illuminate my life, give me for mercy some help.

O blond tresses and well formed face, o great beauty, rare and infinite, give me for mercy some help.

O angelic face, o sweet smile, o sugary and delicious mouth, give me for mercy some help.

I beg you to give me some help, so that I can say that I have my life only from you, infinite beauty.)

[20] Depon l'arco e l'orgoglio

Depon l'arco e l'orgoglio,
Amor, ch'a te non lice
Mai più chiamarti valoros', ardito,
Poich'un' pulce ha ferito
Il bianco petto della mia fenice,

Che già gran tempo sai
Che l'arme spendi, e nol piagasti mai.

(Put down your bow and your pride, Love, for you may never again call yourself bold and daring: a flea has wounded the white breast of my Phoenix, on which, as you know, you have been using your weapons for a long time, and you never wounded it.)

[21] O consiacaldari!

O consiacaldari! Candelieri, fersor', e lucerne da stagnare!
O chi vol consiacaldari? Candelieri, fersor', e lucerne da stagnare!

O spazzacamin!

Caldarrost', caldi, caldi, cott'ades, ades, ades!

Alle beline donne!

Alla bella Franceschina ninina bufina,
La fili bustachina,
Che la vorria mari nininini,
La fili bustachi.

(O tinsmith! Candlesticks, frying pans, and lanterns to tin!
O who wants a tinsmith? Candlesticks, frying pans, and lanterns to tin!

O chimneysweep!

Chestnuts, hot, hot, just cooked!

To the beautiful women!

To the beautiful Franceschina who would like a husband.)

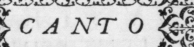

CANTO

IL SECONDO LIBRO
DELLE CANZONI
A SEI VOCI,
DI GIOVAN FERRETTI
Maestro di Capella del Duomo d'Ancona.

Nouamente posti in luce.

IN VINEGGIA.
APPRESSO L'HEREDE DI GIROLAMO SCOTTO
MDLXXV. A

Plate I: Title-page of the Canto partbook of Giovanni Ferretti's *Il secondo libro delle canzoni a sei voci* (Venice: Heirs of Girolamo Scotto, 1575). (Actual size: 21 x 16.2 cm.) (Reproduced by permission of the Bayerische Staatsbibliothek, Munich)

Plate II: Giovanni Ferretti, "O consiacaldari," *mascherata a 8* from *Il secondo libro delle canzoni a sei voci* (Venice: Heirs of Girolamo Scotto, 1575). (Actual size: 21 x 16.2 cm.) (Reproduced by permission of the Bayerische Staatsbibliothek, Munich)

IL SECONDO LIBRO DELLE CANZONI
A SEI VOCI (1575)

[1] Com'al primo apparir

4

6

14

[2] Dolci colli fioriti

19

[3] Voi che te dica

Ch'hai po- chi fat- ti, Ch'hai po- chi fat-

Ch'hai po- chi fat- ti, Ch'hai

n'a- do- na- i Ch'hai po- chi fat- ti, Ch'hai po- chi fat-

n'a- do- na- i Ch'hai po- chi fat- ti, Ch'hai po- chi fat-

n'a- do- na- i Ch'hai po- chi fat- ti, Ch'hai po- chi fat-

n'a- do- na- i Ch'hai po- chi fat- ti,

- ti, Ch'hai po- chi fat- ti, ma___ pa- ro- le as- sa- i.

po- chi fat- ti, ma pa- ro- le as- sa- i.

- ti, Ch'hai po- chi fat- ti, ma pa- ro- le as- sa- i.

- ti, Ch'hai po- chi fat- ti, ma___ pa- ro- le as- sa- i.

- ti, Ch'hai po- chi fat- ti, ma pa- ro- le as- sa- i.

Ch'hai po- chi fat- ti, ma pa- ro- le as- sa- i.

[4] Mirate che m'ha fatto

[5] Ho inteso dir

34

36

[6] Su, su, su, non più dormir

più dor- mir, ché _____ la not- te se ne

non più dor- mir,

- mir, ché la not- te se _____ ne va,

- mir, ché la not- te se _____ ne _____

più dor- mir, ché la not- te se ne va, ché _____

- mir, ché la not- te se _____ ne va,

va, ché la not- te se ne va!

ché la not- te se ne va!

ché la not- te se ne va! Deh _____

va, ché la not- te se ne va! Deh _____

_____ la not- te se _____ ne _____ va! Deh _____

ché la not- te se _____ ne va! Deh _____

[7] Ecco ch'io lass'il core

suo del mio do- lo- - re,_____

- lo- re, del

chi nu- tri- sce il suo del mio_____ do- lo- re, del__

- tri- sce il suo del mio do- lo- -

- lo- re, del mio do- lo-

- tri- sce il suo del mio_____ do-

_ del mio do- lo- re. Deh co-

mio do- lo- re. Deh_____ co-

_ mio do- lo- re. Deh_____ co-

- re, del mio_____ do- lo- re. Deh_____ co-

- re, del mio do- lo- - re.

- lo- - re.

Vi- va del- la mia mor- t'in mag- gior gio-

Vi- va_____ del- la mia mor- t'in mag- gior gio-

- ia Vi-

- ia Vi- va del- la mia mor- t'in mag- gior gio-

- ia

- ia

- ia, Vi- va del- la mia mor- t'in mag- gior gio-

- ia,

- va del- la mia mor- t'in mag- gior_____ gio- ia,

- ia, Vi- va del- la mia mor-

Vi- va del- la mia mor- t'in mag- gior gio-

Vi- va del- la mia mor- t'in mag- gior gio-

[8] Occhi, non occhi

le- ghi, Con sguar- di le- ghi nel lac- cio d'a- mo- re, Con

le- ghi, Con sguar- di le- ghi nel lac- cio d'a- mo- re, Con

sguar- di le- ghi nel_____ lac- cio d'a- mo- re, Con

le- ghi nel lac- cio d'a- mo- re, d'a- mo- re, Con

- ghi, Con sguar- di le- ghi nel_____ lac- cio d'a- mo- re,

le- ghi, Con sguar- di le- ghi nel lac- cio d'a- mo- re, Con

sguar- di le- ghi, Con sguar- di le- ghi, Con sguar-

sguar- di le- ghi, Con sguar- di le-

sguar- di le- ghi, Con sguar- di le- ghi, Con

sguar- di le- ghi, Con sguar- di le- ghi,

Con sguar- di le- ghi, Con sguar- di

sguar- di le- ghi, Con sguar- di le-

[9] Nasce la gioia mia

58

-ro, per- ch'il sguar- -d'è ta-

per- ch'il sguar- d'è ta- le Ch'o-

-ro, per- ch'il sguar- -d'è ta-

-ro, per- ch'il sguar- d'è ta- le Ch'o- gni vol-

-ch'il sguar- d'è ta- le Ch'o-

per- ch'il sguar- d'è ta-

-le Ch'o- gni vol- ta be- a- to

-gni vol- ta, Ch'o- gni vol- ta be- a- to

-le Ch'o- gni vol- ta be- a- to far-

-ta be- a- to far- mi suo- le,

-gni vol- ta be- a- to far- mi, be- a- to far-

-le Ch'o- gni vol- ta be- a- to far-

[10] Un nuovo cacciator

fe- ra Trop- po con fret- t',e non la puol pi- glia-

-gue u- na fe- ra Trop- po con fret- t',e non la puol_____ pi- glia-

__ se- gue u- na fe- ra Trop- po con fret- ta, e non la puol pi- glia-

Trop- po con fret- t',e non la puol pi- glia- re.

- re. No- vel- lo cac- cia-

- re. No- vel- lo cac- cia- tor, sai che voi fa- re? No- vel- lo cac- cia-

- re. No- vel- lo cac- cia- tor,

No- vel- lo cac- cia- tor, sai che voi fa- re?

No- vel- lo cac- cia- tor, sai che voi fa- re? No- vel- lo cac- cia-

No- vel- lo cac- cia- tor, sai che voi fa- re?

dio, ché tu non sai cac- cia- re. Vat- te con dio, ché tu non

dio, ché tu non sai cac- cia- re. Vat- te con dio, ché tu non sai___

sai cac- cia- re. Vat- te con dio, ché tu, ché tu non sai___

sai cac- cia- re. Vat- te con dio, ché tu non

ché tu non sai cac- cia- re. Vat- te con dio, ché tu non

- re, ché tu non sai cac- cia- re. Vat- te con dio, ché tu non sai___

sai cac- cia- re. Vat- te con dio, ché tu non sai cac- cia-

___ cac- cia- re. Vat- - te con dio, Vat- - te con

___ cac- cia- re. Vat- te con dio,

sai cac- cia- re. Vat- te con dio, ché tu___

sai cac- cia- re. Vat- te con dio, ché tu non sai cac- cia- re. Vat-

___ cac- cia- re. Vat- te con dio, ché tu non sai cac- cia- re. Vat-

[11] Ancor che col partir

72

[12] Non è dolor

co- sì vo- glia. Son di- spe- ra- to, Son

co- sì vo- glia. Son di- spe- ra- to, Son di-

- sì vo- glia. Son di- spe- ra- to,_____

co- sì vo- glia. Son di- spe- ra- to, Son di- spe-

- sì vo- glia. Son di- spe- ra- to,

co- sì vo- glia. Son di- spe- ra-

di- spe- ra- to, Son di- spe- ra- to, e

- spe- ra- to, Son di- spe- ra- to,_____

___ Son di- spe- ra- to, e pur mi se-

- ra- to, Son di- spe- ra- to,

Son di- spe- ra- to,

- to, Son di- spe- ra- to,

-mar- mi, Per con- su- mar- mi _____ con

Per con- su- mar- mi con _____ mag-

con- su- mar- mi con mag- gior _____

- mi, Per con- su-mar- mi con _____ mag-

Per con- su- mar- mi con _____ mag-

- mi, Per con- su-mar- mi con _____ mag-

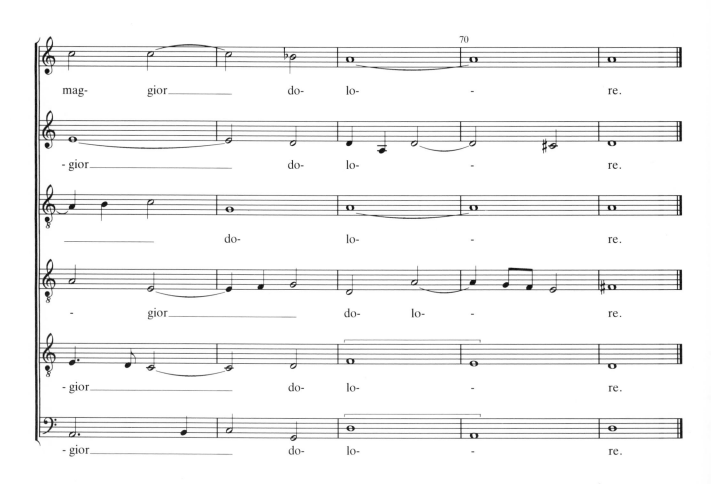

mag- gior _____ do- lo- re.

- gior _____ do- lo- re.

_____ do- lo- re.

- gior _____ do- lo- re.

- gior _____ do- lo- re.

- gior _____ do- lo- re.

[13] O saporito volto

-gli, ti pre- - - - -go il lac- cio, Scio- gli, ti pre- go il lac-

Scio- gli, ti pre- go il lac-

Scio- gli, ti pre- go il lac- cio, Scio- gli, ti pre- go il lac- -

Scio- gli, ti pre- go il lac- cio, Scio- gli, ti pre- go il lac-

Scio- gli, ti pre- go il lac- cio,

Scio- gli, ti pre- go il lac- cio,

- cio, Scio- gli, ti pre- go il lac-

- cio, Scio- gli, ti pre- go il lac- cio, Scio- gli, ti pre- go il lac-

- cio, Scio- gli, ti pre- go il lac- cio:

- cio,_____ Scio- gli, ti pre- go il lac-

Scio- gli, ti pre- go il lac- cio:

Scio- gli, ti pre- go il lac- cio:

[14] Ognun s'allegra

[15] Occhi leggiadri

Canto: Oc- chi leg- gia- dri, do- - v'a- mor fa ni- do, do- v'a- mor fa

Alto: Oc- chi leg- gia- dri, do- - v'a- mor fa ni- do, do- - v'a- mor fa

Sesto: Oc- chi leg- gia- dri, do- - v'a- mor fa ni- do,

Quinto: Oc- chi leg- gia- dri, do- - v'a- mor fa

Tenore: Oc- chi leg- gia- dri, do- - v'a- mor fa

Basso: Oc- chi leg- gia- dri, do- - v'a- mor fa ni- do,

ni- do, ni- do, Ché tan- ti stral ad im- - pia- gar- mi il

ni- do, ni- do, Ché tan- ti stral___ ad im- pia- gar- mi il___

Ché tan- ti stral ad___ im- pia- gar- mi il co-

ni- do, ni- do, Ché tan- ti stral ad im- pia- gar- mi il

ni- do, ni- do, Ché tan- ti stral ad im- - pia- gar- mi il

Ché tan- ti stral ad im- - pia- gar- mi il

co- re, ad___ im- pia- gar- mi il co- re?_____ Che

___ co- re, ad im- pia- gar- mi il co- re? Che gio- va sa- et- tar,___

- re, ad im- pia- gar- mi il co- re? Che gio- va

co- re? Che gio- va sa- et- tar,

co- re?

co- re? Che gio- va sa- et-

gio- va sa- et- tar, Che gio- va sa-

___ Che gio- va sa- - et- tar, Che gio- va

sa- et- tar, Che gio- va sa- et- tar, Che gio- va

Che gio- - va sa- et- tar, Che gio- va sa- et-

Che gio- va sa- et- tar, Che gio- va sa- et- tar,

- tar, Che gio- va sa- et- tar,

et- tar, Che gio- va sa- et- tar un che si mo- re?
che si mo- re, Che gio- va sa- et- tar un che si mo- re?
gio- va sa- et- tar un che si mo- re?
- va sa- et- tar, Che gio- va sa- et- tar un che si mo- re?
- tar, Che gio- va sa- et- tar un che si mo- re?
sa- et- tar, Che gio- va sa- et- tar un che si mo- re?

[16] Qual donna canterà

Qual don- na can- te- rà, se non can- t'i- o, Qual
se non can- t'i- o, Qual
Qual don- na can- te- rà, se non can-

100

Seconda parte

110

- co, si- gnor mi- o.

- co, te- co, si- gnor mi- o.

te- co, si- gnor mi- o.

- co, si- gnor mi- o.

te- co, si- gnor mi- o.

mi- o, te- co, si- gnor mi- o.

Terza parte

È ch'io li piac- cio,

E quel ch'in que-sto m'è som- mo pia- ce- re È ch'io li piac- cio, È

E quel ch'in que- sto m'è som-mo pia- ce- re È

E quel ch'in que- sto m'è som-mo pia- ce- re,

È ch'io li piac-

È ch'io li piac-

[17] Bon cacciator

- tor giam- mai non per- se cac- cia,

cia, Bon cac- cia- tor giam-

Bon cac- cia- tor giam- mai non per- se cac-

Bon cac- cia- tor giam- mai non per- se cac- cia,

cac- cia- tor giam- mai non per- se cac- cia,

Bon cac- cia- tor giam- mai non

Bon cac- cia- tor giam- mai non

- mai non per- se cac- cia, giam-

cia, Bon cac- cia- tor giam-

giam- mai non per- se cac- cia.

Bon cac- cia- tor giam- mai non

per- se cac- cia, giam- mai non

118

[18] Mettetevi in battaglia

- mor, E con-tr'a- mor, E con-tr'a- mor an- da-te tut-t'in fret-

- mor, E con-tr'a- mor an- da-te tut-t'in fret- ta,

E con-tr'a- mor, E con- tr'a- mor_____ an- da-te tut-t'in fret-

- mor, E con-tr'a- mor an- da-te tut-t'in fret- ta,

E con-tr'a- mor, E con- tr'a- mor an- da-te tut-t'in fret-

E con-tr'a- mor, E con-tr'a- mor an- da-te tut-t'in fret-

- ta, Ch'in po- co spa- zio ne fa-

Ch'in po- co spa- zio, Ch'in po- co spa- zio

- ta, Ch'in po- co spa- zio

Ch'in po- co spa- zio

- ta, Ch'in po- co spa- zio

- ta, Ch'in po- co spa- zio

- zio ne fa- rò ven- det- ta, ne fa- rò ven- det- ta,

Ch'in po- co spa- zio ne fa- rò ven- det- ta, ne fa- rò ven-

- zio, Ch'in po- co spa- zio ne fa- rò ven- det- ta,

spa- zio ne fa- rò

- zio ne fa- rò ven- det- ta, ne

Ch'in po- co spa- zio ne fa- rò ven- det- ta,

ne fa- rò, ne fa- rò ven- det- ta, ne fa- rò ven- det- ta.

- det- ta, ne fa- rò ven- det- ta, ne fa- rò ven- det- ta.

ne fa- rò, ne fa- rò, ne fa- rò ven- det- ta.

ven- det- ta, ne fa- rò ven- det- ta.

fa- rò, ne fa- rò, ne fa- rò ven- det- ta.

ne fa- rò, ne fa- rò, ne fa- rò, ne fa- rò ven- det- ta.

[19] O faccia che rallegri

-ge- te- mi di_____ gra- zia qual- che a- i- ta,

-zia, Por- ge- te- mi di gra- - zia qual- - che a- i-

-ta, qual- che a- i-

Por- ge- te- mi di gra- zia,

-ge- te- mi di gra- zia qual- che a- i-

Por- ge- te- mi di gra- zia qual- - che a- i-

Por- ge- te- mi di gra- zia qual- - che a- i- ta.

-ta, Por- ge- te- mi di gra- zia qual- - che a- i- - ta.

-ta, Por- ge- te- mi di gra- - zia qual- - che a- i- ta.

Por- ge- te- mi di gra- zia qual- - che a- i- ta.

-ta, Por- ge- te- mi di gra- zia qual- - che a- i- ta.

-ta, Por- ge- te- mi di gra- zia qual- - che a- i- ta.

[20] Depon l'arco e l'orgoglio

136

va- lo- ro- s',ar- di- to, Mai più chia- mar- ti va- lo-

-ro- s',ar- di- to, Mai più chia- mar- ti,

va- lo- ro- s',ar- di- to, Mai più chia- mar- ti va-

va- lo- ro- s',ar- di- to, Mai più chia-

-di- to, Mai più chia- mar- ti va- lo- ro-

va- lo- ro- s',ar- di- to, Mai più chia- mar- ti,

-ro- s',ar- di- to, Mai più chia- mar- ti va- lo-

Mai più chia- mar- ti va- lo- ro- s',ar-

- lo- ro- s',ar- di- to,

-mar- ti, Mai più chia- mar- ti va- lo-

- so, Mai più chia- mar- ti va- lo- ro- s',ar-

Mai più chia- mar- ti va- lo-

[21] O consiacaldari!

Appendix:
CANZONE MODELS

[2a] Dolci colli fioriti

Poiché quei raggi suoi sono sì chiari,
Perché nel giorno a me mandan la sera?
Deh fatemi un favore:
Diteli che mi moro di dolore.

Se saranno ver me cotanto avari,
Saranno ancor cagion che presto io pera.
Deh fatemi un favore:
Diteli che mi moro di dolore.

Per acquetar gli ardenti miei sospiri,
Dicovi la cagion di miei martiri.
Deh fatemi un favore:
Diteli che mi moro di dolore.

150

[8a] Occhi, non occhi

[Anonymous]

Non sono labbra queste labbra belle;
Son gioie e perle, e di corall'il core,
Che or vita, or morte, dona a tutte l'ore.

Non furo al mondo sì belle mammelle,
Che a noi stillasse sì dolce liquore,
Che per gustar'al mondo non si more.

Quess'occhi foron ch'allaccio d'amore
Al primo sguardo mi legar'il core,
Che vive in morte, e nella vita more.

[11a] Ancor che col partir

Gasparo Fiorino

Perché se nel partir l'alma s'accora,
Non sente nel tornar gravosi omei,
Tanto son dolci gli ritorni miei.

E se giungo partendo all'ultim'ora,
Mi pone il ritornar vivo fra i Dei,
Tanto son dolci gli ritorni miei.

Così sento la morte e vita quando
Da voi mi parto e poi faccio ritorno,
Sol contemplando questo viso adorno.

[13a] O saporito volto

Marc'Antonio Mazzone

O bianca e bella mano,
Per te son fatto insano.
Or sciogli le catene:
Dammi la libertà; non vo' più pene.

O delicato aspetto,
Ho perso l'intelletto.
Dammi la libertade,
Poiché sei bella, e mostri crudeltade.

S'io vedo sciolto il laccio,
Sarò fuora d'impaccio.
S'io sciolgo le catene,
Vivo contento, e poi beato mene.

[14a] Ognun s'allegra

Canto

Tenore

Basso

Marc'Antonio Mazzone

O- gnun s'al-le- gra e vi-v'in fes-t'e in gio- co, in fes-t'e in gio- co,

gio- co; S'al- le-gra il ciel, la ter- ra, ed o- gni fio- re, Quan- d'e-sci, o chia-ro

so- le, Quan- d'e-sci, o chia-ro sol, col tuo splen- do- re, do- re.

Bellezza e leggiadria in ogni loco
Si vede, e par che là ci regna amore,
Quand'esci, o chiaro sol, col tuo splendore.

Ognun che viv'in amoroso foco
Si sent'alleviar ogni dolore,
Quand'esci, o chiaro sol, col tuo splendore.

Ed io, che per te vivo in gran martire,
Subito mi si rasserena il core,
Quand'esci, o chiaro sol, col tuo splendore.

[15a] Occhi leggiadri

Moro di dolor, piangendo rido,
Ma di mia mort'ovunque regn'amore
Non te ne può venir largo onore.

Onor sarebb'a te, crudel'infido,
S'è ver ch'hai fra li Dei forz'e valore,
Temprar'in part'il mio profund'ardore,

Non con dui occh'il cuor sempre impiagarme.
Vita non ho con che possa aitarme.
Vedi ch'io moro omai; che puoi tu farme?

[17a] Bon cacciator

[Anonymous]

L'agresta con lo tempo fa guarnaccia.
Pian piano s'ammaturano l'olive;
Però voglio seguir perfin che viva.

Press'al mal tempo viene la bonaccia.
Da uno sdegno grand'amor deriva;
Però voglio seguir perfin che viva.

Non vale per combatter una maglia,
E fuggir sempre incontr'alla battaglia,
Ch'al fin la donna vole della quaglia.

[19a] O faccia che rallegri

[Anonymous]

O treccie bionde e ben compiuto viso,
O gran beltade rara ed infinita,
Porgetimi di grazia qualche aita.

O viso angelicato, o dolce riso,
O bocca inzuccherata e saporita,
Porgetimi di grazia qualche aita.

Vi prego mi porgeti qualche aita,
Acciò possa anco dir, che questa vita,
L'abbia sola da voi, beltà infinita.